# The Three Little Pigs

Illustrated by
Georgien Overwater

Retold by Susanna Davidson

Once upon a time,
there were three little pigs.

They lived with their mother in a snug little house...

until the little pigs grew **too big**.

"It's time you found homes of your own,"
said their mother.

So off they trotted, on their short pink legs.

Trottity-trot,

trottity-trot,

trottity-trot.

"Watch out for the big bad wolf,"
called Mother Pig.

Soon, they met a man selling straw.

"Ooh!" squealed the first little pig.
"May I buy some?"

"I'm going to build
a straw house,"
he announced.

He set to work right away.

His house had four straw walls,

a neat straw floor,

a fine straw roof,

and a
stylish
straw
door.

"Isn't it grand?" said the first little pig.
The others weren't so sure.
They muttered and tutted, then trotted away.

Soon, they met a man selling sticks.

"Ooh!" squealed the second little pig. "May I buy some?"

"I'm going to build a stick house," he said proudly.

Sticks for Sale

"Isn't my house grand?
Sticks are better than straw."

The third little pig wasn't so sure.

She trotted on, until...

Bricks
for sale

Bricks
for sale

...she found some bricks.

"Ooh! Please may I buy
some?" she asked.
"I'm going to build
a brick house."

BUY
BRICKS
HERE

Bricks
for sale

"Brick houses
are the best
of all."

The next day, the big bad wolf
came to the straw house.
"Little pig, little pig, let me in!"
he called.

"Not by the hair on
my chinny chin chin,"
said the first little pig.

"Then I'll **huff**, and I'll
**puff** and I'll BLOW
your house in."

The wolf **huffed**

and he **puffed**...

...and he BLEW
the house in.

The little pig ran as fast as he could to the stick house. The wolf was right behind him.

"Little pigs, little pigs, let me in!" cried the wolf.

"Not by the hair
on our chinny chin chins!"
cried the two little pigs.

"Then I'll **huff** and I'll **puff** and I'll BLOW your house in."

And he **huffed**...

and he **puffed**...

...until, at last, he BLEW the house in.

The little pigs ran as fast as they could to the brick house.
The wolf was just behind them.

"Little pigs, little pigs, let me in!"

"No!" yelled the three little pigs.
"Not by the hair on our chinny chin chins!"

"Then I'll **huff** and I'll **puff** and I'll BLOW your house in!"
cried the wolf.

And he **huffed** and he **puffed**
and he **huffed** and he **puffed**.

Huff

Puff

Huff

He **huffed** and he **puffed** until...

PUFF

Huff

...he ran out of **puff**.

"Hee, hee, hee!" laughed
the three little pigs.
"You can't get in!"

But the wolf jumped
onto the roof.

He slid down
the chimney

and landed, SPLOSH,
in the cooking pot.

The third little pig
picked up the lid...

...and all three slammed it on.
"By the hair on our chinny chin chins," they said,
"we won't be seeing that wolf again!"

Edited by Jenny Tyler and Lesley Sims
Designed by Caroline Spatz
Cover design by Louise Flutter

First published in 2011 by Usborne Publishing Ltd, 83-85 Saffron Hill, London EC1N 8RT, England.
www.usborne.com Copyright © 2011, 2008 Usborne Publishing Ltd. The name Usborne and the devices ♆ ⊕ are Trade Marks
of Usborne Publishing Ltd. All rights reserved. No part of this publication may be reproduced, stored in a retrieval system,
or transmitted in any form or by any means, electronic, mechanical, photocopying, recording or otherwise,
without the prior permission of the publisher. First published in America in 2011. UE.